NOT JUST ANY RING

by Danita Ross Haller

pictures by Deborah Kogan Ray

Alfred A. Knopf
New York

THIS IS A BORZOI BOOK PUBLISHED BY ALFRED A. KNOPF, INC.

Copyright © 1982 by Danita Ross Haller
Illustrations Copyright © 1982 by Deborah Kogan Ray
All rights reserved under International and Pan-American
Copyright Conventions. Published in the United States
by Alfred A. Knopf, Inc., New York, and simultaneously in
Canada by Random House of Canada Limited, Toronto.
Distributed by Random House, Inc., New York.
Designed by Mimi Harrison
Manufactured in the United States of America
10 9 8 7 6 5 4 3 2 1

Library of Congress Cataloging in Publication Data
Haller, Danita Ross. Not just any ring.
Summary: Jessie's grandfather buys her a special silver ring,
but she must depend on the magic in her heart and the
strength in her hands when she and her grandfather
are stranded in the desert.
[1. Survival—Fiction.   2. Grandfathers—Fiction.
3. Indians of North America—Fiction]
I. Ray, Deborah, ill. II. Title.
PZ7.H1543No   1982   [Fic]   81-14242
ISBN 0-394-85082-3   AACR2
ISBN 0-394-95082-8 (lib. bdg.)

For those of us who sometimes wish for magic.

To Angela and Michelle, D.R.H.

To Frances, D.K.R.

Jessie Yano wants a ring.
But not just any ring.

Jessie Yano wants a ring
like Nellie Sena's.
Nellie Sena's ring is silver
with a smooth, flat,
polished black stone.
And in the center
of the stone
there is a tiny silver dove.
So tiny
almost no one notices.
But Jessie Yano notices.

And Jessie Yano knows
something else
about that ring.
She knows it is a magic ring.
When Nellie Sena
wears that silver ring,
she has good days.

Nellie Sena told her about that ring—
how it came from the mission shop,
and how an old man in a long brown robe
blessed it.
That's why the ring brings good days for her.

Today everything was wrong
for Jessie Yano.
Now as she walks the mesa path
to her home,
she wishes like anything
for a silver ring
with a black stone
and a tiny silver dove.
She holds her hands out in front of her
and imagines that ring
on her finger.
She knows how good it would feel
and how proud she would be
to have her own silver ring.

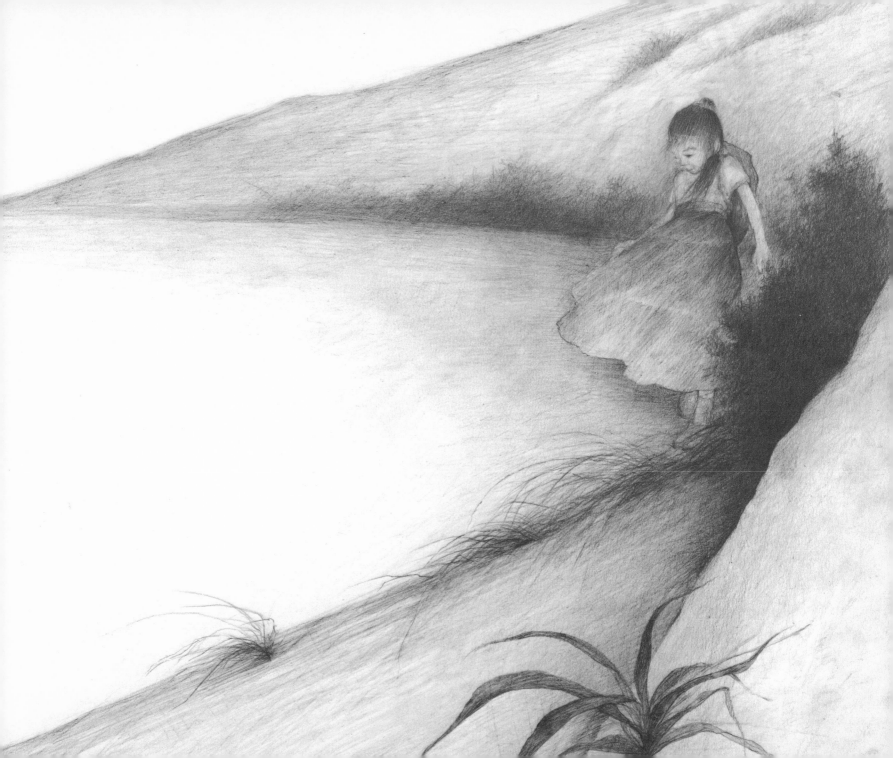

Jessie Yano's grandfather
sits by the path
waiting for Jessie.
She sees him now;
sees his green flannel shirt
and a green flannel arm
waving high in the air.
She hurries to meet him.

Jessie sits awhile
by her grandfather.
They talk of the day.

Grandfather tells
of the sculpture he works at.
Slowly, slowly
in his workshop
every day,
he chips away at stone.
One day,
when he has chipped away enough,
the block of stone
will be a beautiful face.

Jessie looks at her grandfather's hands.
Strong hands, skilled hands.
She tries to imagine
that silver ring
on those fingers,
but can't.

Now she speaks of what is on her mind,
the only thing that is on her mind.
"Grandfather, I need a ring.
I need a silver ring like Nellie Sena's,
a silver ring to bring good days."
"And does Nellie Sena's silver ring
bring her good days?"

"Yes, Grandfather,
it always brings her good days.
The ring came from the mission shop.
It was blessed
especially to bring good days."

"Ahhh." Grandfather nods;
his eyes look far away.
No more is said about the ring this day.

But Jessie Yano
does not forget the silver ring.
She cannot forget it.

She makes paper rings
and clay rings
and ribbon rings.
But they are not
that silver ring.
It's that silver ring she needs.

One day
as Jessie walks the worn path home,
her grandfather waits for her
in the white pickup truck.
He motions for Jessie to get in.
"Where are we going?" Jessie asks.
"It is a surprise, Jessie.
A surprise for you."

They drive slowly
down off the mesa
and into the desert country.
The road winds
and twists
and turns
for some time.

At last
Jessie sees
the old brown mission church.
She looks at her grandfather.
He smiles,
and Jessie hopes she is right
about this surprise.

Jessie Yano and her grandfather
walk together
to the door of a small shop
at the side of the mission church.
Little glass chimes tinkle
as the wooden door opens.

Inside it is dim and cool
and smells of candles and
earthen walls.
Jessie sees shelves
of colorful statues
and vases.

Then she sees a glass counter.
And behind the glass,
on the top shelf,
she sees the rings.

"Here, Grandfather,
here they are," Jessie whispers excitedly.
A lady with a kind face
slides back the glass door
and takes out the tray.
There are many different rings.
Jessie looks up one row
and down another.
Finally
Jessie sees
one silver ring
with a smooth, flat,
polished black stone.
In the center of the stone
there is a tiny silver dove.

Jessie lifts the ring
out of the tray
and slides it onto her finger.
It is beautiful.

She looks at her grandfather.
He nods his head yes.
It is hers.

Jessie stops as they walk out
toward the truck.
"Grandfather, I need my ring blessed."
"I don't believe there is anyone here
to bless it today, Jessie."
"But it must be blessed!
Can't you bless it, Grandfather?"

Grandfather stoops down
and takes her hands in his.
"I cannot bless your ring, Jessie,
but together we might make a prayer
for the ring and for good days."

"Yes, I would like that," says Jessie.

"Jessie, before we make a prayer
I must say some things to you of magic
and of good days.

When I take a stone and shape it
into a deer, or a bird, or a face,
you often say
that my hands must be magic.
I say to you now, Jessie,
that my hands are my tools,
only my tools.
Any magic is within my heart.
If you believe in something
with your heart,
then it can be yours.
If you believe this will be
a good ring for you,
then it will be.
If you believe in good days,
then they will come.
Always,
the real magic
is within your heart."

Jessie Yano sits beside her grandfather
on an old wooden bench
outside the mission church.
Together
they make a prayer for the ring
and for good days.
Then they drive toward home.

The old truck comes to the fork
in the road at the bottom of the great mesa.
To the left
the road climbs slowly until it becomes
a rim on the side of the mesa.
This is the road everyone travels.

To the right
the road veers off into the canyon
and wanders for some miles
before climbing the mesa.
This is the old road, a longer trip
and difficult in some places.
But it is beautiful in the canyon,
especially at sunset.
This is the road
Jessie and her grandfather like the best.
She is glad
when the truck turns to the right,
into the canyon.

The old dirt road
is rutted and bumpy.
But Jessie does not mind.
She sees only the setting sun,
thinks only of her silver ring.

The white truck comes to a sudden stop.
Directly in front of them
the road dips into a sandy arroyo.
The sand will be soft this time of year,
and Grandfather is not certain
the truck can make it across.
"We can make it, Grandfather,
sure we can," Jessie says.
Grandfather backs the truck down the road
and then starts forward as fast as he can.
They hit the arroyo.
The wheels slide,
then straighten and race forward.
Suddenly, the back tires spin,
and the truck stops.
Grandfather and Jessie climb out
to have a look.
The wheels are buried in the sand.
"We are certainly stuck," Grandfather says.
Grandfather's face is serious
as he looks at the sky.
The sun is sinking low.

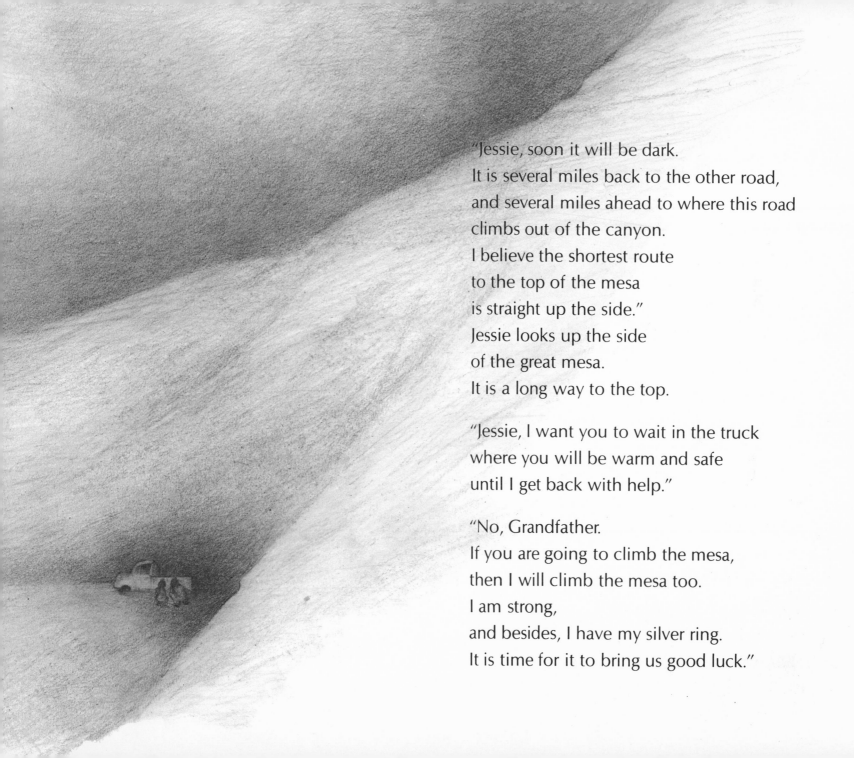

"Jessie, soon it will be dark.
It is several miles back to the other road,
and several miles ahead to where this road
climbs out of the canyon.
I believe the shortest route
to the top of the mesa
is straight up the side."
Jessie looks up the side
of the great mesa.
It is a long way to the top.

"Jessie, I want you to wait in the truck
where you will be warm and safe
until I get back with help."

"No, Grandfather.
If you are going to climb the mesa,
then I will climb the mesa too.
I am strong,
and besides, I have my silver ring.
It is time for it to bring us good luck."

Together they start
up the side of the great mesa.
It is difficult to climb.
Rocks and boulders jut out everywhere.
Several times Jessie slips.
Then Grandfather slips.
Only one time, but it is a bad slip.
Grandfather's ankle turns and twists.
He drops to his knees in pain.

They examine the ankle.
It is already starting to swell.
Grandfather tries to stand, but can't.
It is too painful.
He sits, resting his head in his hands.
Jessie stands very still.
Fear crawls slowly up her body,
making her shiver.

Finally Grandfather speaks.
"Jessie, now you must be a mountain goat.
Take your magic ring
and climb to the top of the mesa for help."

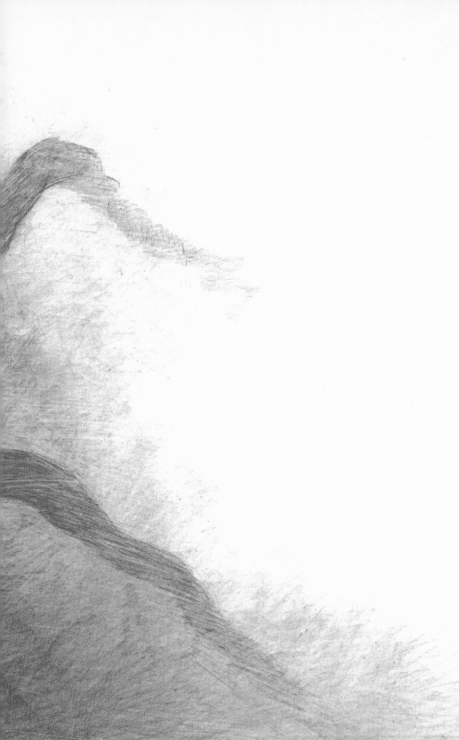

Jessie looks at her grandfather.
Tears blur her eyes.
"Grandfather, I can't leave you here alone."

"Jessie, I will be fine. Remember,
I am quite at home
among these rocks and stones.
You must go and get help
while there is still light."

Jessie's heart pounds hard against her chest.
How can these things happen
now that she has her silver ring?
She looks at the ring.
"This is not a magic ring.
It is not even a good ring.
I hate it!"
She pulls the ring off her finger
and throws it to the ground.

Jessie clings to her grandfather
for a moment
and then begins the long climb
up the mesa.

Looking up,
Jessie picks out a lone juniper tree
at the very top of the mesa.
She will not lose sight of that tree.
She will touch that tree.

Stumbling now,
she plunges forward.
Dried brush scratches at her legs
and snags her clothing.
Rocks slip beneath her feet.
Still she pushes upward,
watching that tree.
Soon she is breathing hard and fast.
Her throat is dry.
The mesa seems to swallow her,
but the tree is closer, a little closer.

Jessie moves on,
crawling and climbing the mesa
like a little worm.

The mesa stands above her
like a wall.
This is the steepest part of the climb,
and the sandy soil
makes it hard to get a good hold.
Small trees grow straight out into the air.
The first one Jessie reaches for
comes out by its roots.
Jessie slides down, down,
until she catches herself on a vine.
She clings there,
against the side of the mesa,
her body shaking,
her fingers and feet dug into the earth.

She closes her eyes.
She cannot move even one more inch.
She thinks she may die
right there on the side of the mesa.
Then she opens her eyes
and sees her hands.
She wishes now that she had that silver ring.
She wishes she had given it one more chance.
She wishes she had even a little magic.
Jessie remembers her grandfather
somewhere below her, waiting.
She remembers about the magic in his heart.
She hears his words about believing with your heart.
But all her heart can do is pound.

She thinks of her grandfather's strong hands.
She is his granddaughter.
She has strong hands too.
Suddenly she wants her hands to work,
to pull her up,
up to the top of the mesa.
She wants it more than anything in the world.
She watches her hands.
They are moving, reaching, grabbing,
digging into the earth.
Her feet follow,
digging, pushing, climbing.

She talks to the mesa.
Talks to the trees.
Talks to anything that might hear her
as she scrambles and slides and reaches
and finally pulls herself to the top
of the great mesa.

Jessie Yano lies exhausted
on the flat earth of the mesa top—
but only for a moment.
Then she jumps up.

The sun has set.
She cannot see the truck
or her grandfather
down in the canyon.
But she waves a juniper limb
and hollers that she is safe.
Then she runs toward the lights of houses
that dot the mesa.
She runs for help.

Much later,
riding in a truck,
Jessie Yano arrives back in the canyon
with friends.
She sees her grandfather
sitting near his truck
by a small fire.
Jessie runs to him
and throws both arms around him.

"Grandfather, how did you get back down here?"
"I made a staff out of a tree limb
and managed to scoot back down.
But it is not so special that I made it
to the bottom of the mesa, Jessie.
What is special
is that you made it to the top."

Jessie Yano looks up at the mesa.
Even in the darkness
its great shape
looms toward the sky.
She had climbed it all right.
She guesses
she had some of that magic
after all.
The real magic
that is in the heart.

"Jessie," Grandfather speaks softly.
"I have something for you."
He opens his hands.
There, in the palm of one hand,
is the silver ring.

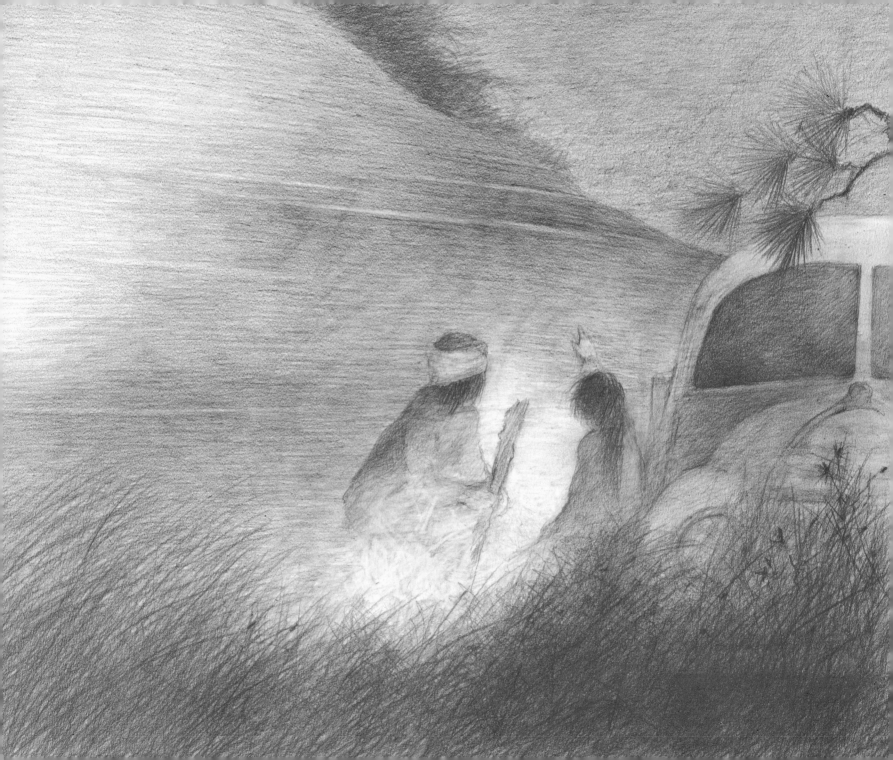

Jessie takes the ring
and slides it back onto her finger.
She thinks of how good it feels.
Now she watches
as the white truck is towed out of the arroyo.
Suddenly
she feels very happy
about this day.

It has been a good day after all.

DANITA ROSS HALLER
loves the land she writes about—
with its Spanish and Indian
influences, and diverse cultures
and traditions. She studied at
the University of Missouri and
is now working toward a degree in
Journalism at the University of
New Mexico. She has two daughters
and lives in Santa Fe.

DEBORAH KOGAN RAY
is a well known illustrator and
award-winning artist whose work has
been widely exhibited. Nature
and the outdoors are often the
subject of her paintings, and she
shares Ms. Haller's love for
the mesas of the Southwest. She has
two daughters and lives in
Philadelphia.